A NOTE TO PARENTS

When your children are ready to "step into reading," giving them the right books—and lots of them—is as crucial as giving them the right food to eat. **Step into Reading Books** present exciting stories and information reinforced with lively, colorful illustrations that make learning to read fun, satisfying, and worthwhile. They are priced so that acquiring an entire library of them is affordable. And they are beginning readers with an important difference—they're written on four levels.

Step 1 Books, with their very large type and extremely simple vocabulary, have been created for the very youngest readers. **Step 2 Books** are both longer and slightly more difficult. **Step 3 Books,** written to mid-second-grade reading levels, are for the child who has acquired even greater reading skills. **Step 4 Books** offer exciting nonfiction for the increasingly proficient reader.

Children develop at different ages. **Step into Reading Books,** with their four levels of reading, are designed to help children become good—and interested—readers *faster*. The grade levels assigned to the four steps—preschool through grade 1 for Step 1, grades 1 through 3 for Step 2, grades 2 and 3 for Step 3, and grades 2 through 4 for Step 4—are intended only as guides. Some children move through all four steps very rapidly; others climb the steps over a period of several years. These books will help your child "step into reading" in style!

Sir Small and

To Robby, who thought up the idea for this book

Library of Congress Cataloging-in-Publication Data:
O'Connor, Jane. Sir Small and the dragonfly / by Jane O'Connor ; illustrated by John O'Brien.   p.   cm.—(Step into reading. A Step 1 b[...]
SUMMARY: When a dragonfly swoops over the town of Pee Wee and carries Lady Teena away, brave Sir Small rides off on his trusty ant vow[...]
to rescue her.   ISBN 0-394-89625-4 (trade); ISBN 0-394-99625-9 (lib. bdg.)   [1. Knights and knighthood—Fiction. 2. Size—Ficti[...]
I. O'Brien, John, 1953– ill. II. Title. III. Series: Step into reading. Step 1 book. PZ7.0222Si 1988 [E]—dc19 87-35309

Manufactured in the United States of America   26 27 28 29 30

STEP INTO READING is a trademark of Random House, Inc.

he Dragonfly

By Jane O'Connor
Illustrated by John O'Brien

A Step 1 Book

Random House 🏠 New York

Long, long ago
a tiny knight rode
his trusty ant
into the town of Pee Wee.

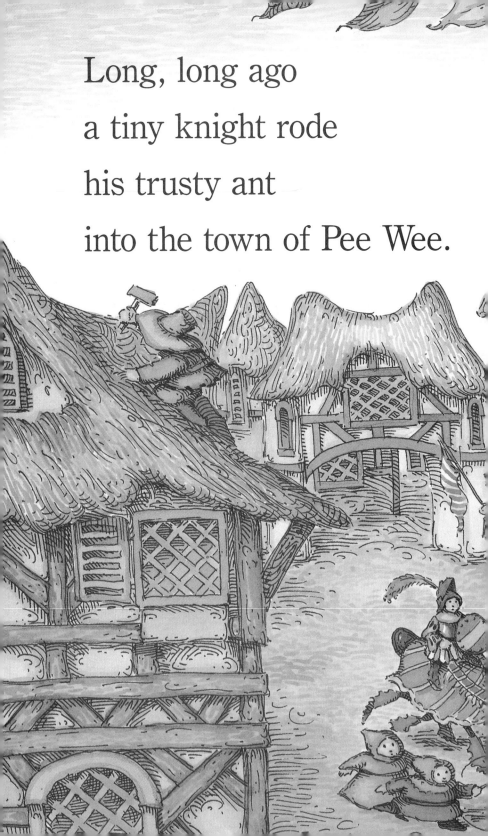

In Pee Wee
the tallest person was
no taller than a toothpick.
The biggest house was
no bigger than a shoe box.

"This is the town for me!"
said the tiny knight.
"I think I will stay here."
And so he did.

But one day
a dragonfly flew over the town.
"Run for your lives!"
cried the people of Pee Wee.

Lady Teena ran.

Down came the dragonfly.

WHOOSH!

Up went Lady Teena.

"Help! Help!" she shouted.

"The dragonfly has taken
Lady Teena to its cave.
Who can save her?"
asked the king.

The butcher said,
"I am too old."

The baker said,
"I am too fat."

The candlestick maker said,
"I am too scared."

"I am not scared,"
said the tiny knight.
"You? Who are you?"
asked the king.
"I am Sir Small.
I have my sword."
It was the size of a pin.
"I have my shield."
It was no bigger
than a penny.
"And I have my trusty ant."

The king laughed.
"You are even smaller
than we are!"

"I am small,
but I am brave.
I will save Lady Teena."

Sir Small rode to the cave
of the dragonfly.

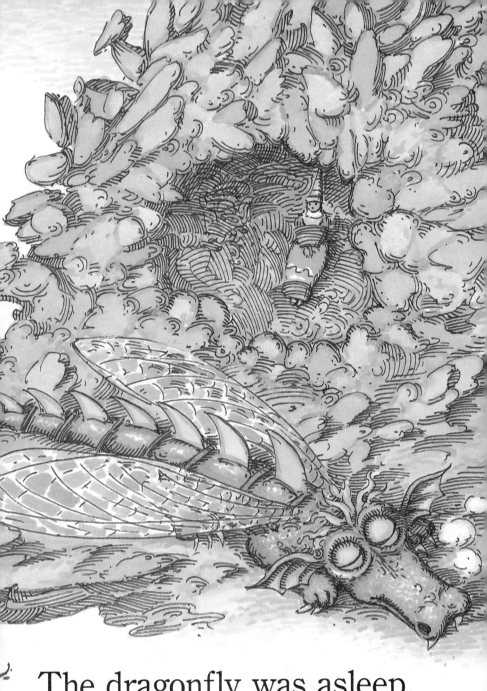

The dragonfly was asleep.

Lucky Sir Small!

"Shh!" he said
to Lady Teena.
Then he cut the ropes.
Lady Teena was free!
"Come with me,"
Sir Small told her.

Lady Teena got on
Sir Small's ant.
Away they rode.
There was no time to lose!

Soon the dragonfly woke up.
Where was the pretty lady?
The dragonfly wanted
her back.

The dragonfly flew
after Sir Small
and Lady Teena.
It came closer and closer.

But Sir Small
was not scared.
He saw a big spider web.
Now he had a plan!

Sir Small rode
behind the web.
"Try and get us!"
he called to the dragonfly.

Down came the dragonfly.
It flew into the web
and was trapped.
That was the end
of the dragonfly!

That night
the people of Pee Wee
had a big party.

Lady Teena
sat with Sir Small.
They were very happy.

The king said,
"Here's to Sir Small.
The smallest—
but bravest—of all!"